by David Mack

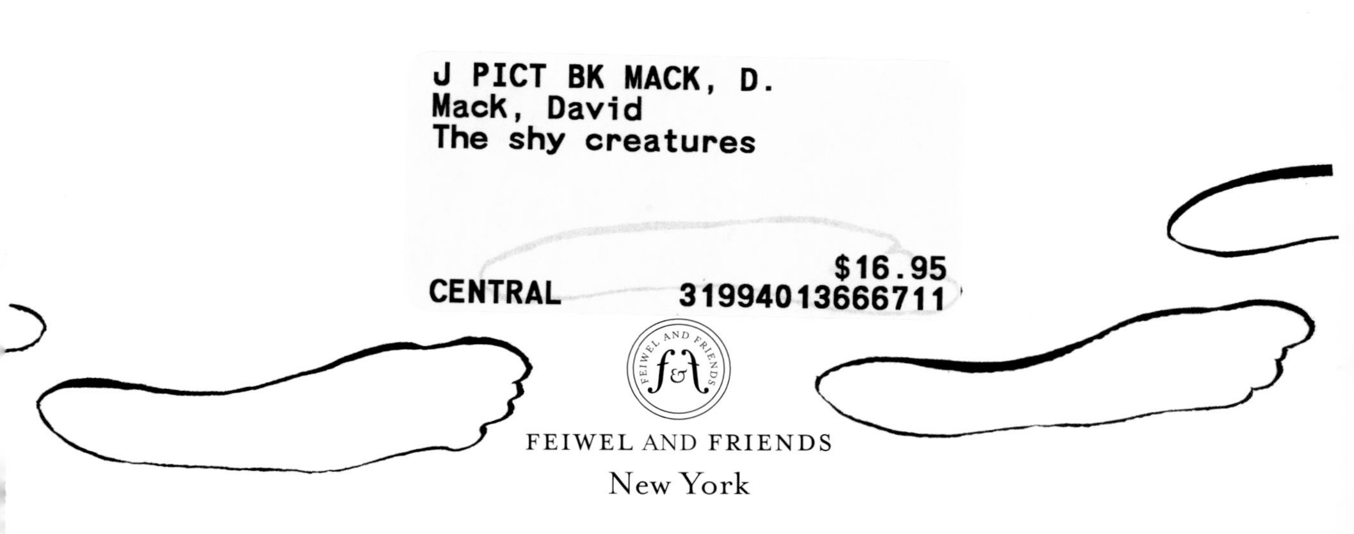

FEIWEL AND FRIENDS
New York

About the Creatures

- **ABOMINABLE SNOWMAN**: A native of the Himalayas, the Abominable Snowman, also known as the Yeti, has been sighted by climbers of Mount Everest for decades.
- **BIGFOOT**: Similar in appearance to his cousin the Yeti, the Bigfoot, or Sasquatch, is most commonly sighted in the western regions of the United States and Canada.
- **CHUPACABRA**: In Spanish, *El Chupacabra* means "the goat sucker." In the early 1990s in Puerto Rico, when dead animals were being found by farmers, the Chupacabra myth expanded out to other parts of Latin America in the form of a hybrid animal crossbred from aliens, dinosaurs, porcupines, kangaroos, and other unlikely animals.
- **CYCLOPS**: The Cyclops was believed to be a member of a race of giants with a large, single eye in the middle of his forehead, according to Greek mythology.
- **DRAGON**: Known in the west as a scaly, winged, fire-breathing lizard, the dragon is said to hoard treasure and kill anyone who tries to steal it. In the east, the dragon is portrayed as a benevolent, powerful, intelligent creature with a serpentine, wingless body and without the ability to breathe fire.
- **GREY ALIENS**: Short, slender, and delicate, Grey Aliens' hairless, oversized heads and large, lidless, black eyes have become quite familiar because they are depicted as the typical alien in pop culture.
- **LOCH NESS MONSTER**: Hunted for more than a century, sighted by dozens of witnesses, the Loch Ness Monster lives in one of three large lochs in northern Scotland. "Nessie" is believed to be a large, finned, perhaps prehistoric, aquatic creature with a long, curved neck.
- **PEGASUS**: In Greek mythology, the Pegasus is the white, winged horse sired by Medusa and Poseidon, the god of the sea.
- **PHOENIX**: A legendary creature from Egyptian and Greek mythology, the phoenix sings a song so beautiful, the sun-god stops to listen. One of a kind, at the end of its life, the phoenix builds a nest of wood and sets itself on fire only to rise out of the ashes – reborn anew.
- **PUSHMI-PULLYU**: Invented by Hugh Lofting for his Doctor Doolittle books, the pushmi-pullyu is a two-headed herbivorous member of the deer family that uses one head for speaking, and the other for eating. Also, each head takes turns sleeping since the pushmi-pullyu is very shy and keeps watch to prevent being spotted or captured.
- **UNICORN**: The unicorn's legend exists in numerous cultures and incarnations throughout history. A white horse with a spiraled horn, a virtuous nature, and the power to heal is its most commonly depicted form.

Special thanks to Allen Spiegel and Liz Szabla,
and colorful Shy Creature Anh Tran.

A FEIWEL AND FRIENDS BOOK
An Imprint of Holtzbrinck Publishers

For information, address Feiwel and Friends, 175 Fifth Avenue, New York, N.Y., 10010.

Library of Congress Cataloging-in-Publication Data

Mack, David
The Shy Creatures / David Mack.—1st ed. p. cm.
I. Title. PS3613.A272546 2007 811'.6—dc22 2006036340
ISBN-13: 978-0-312-36794-7 • ISBN-10: 0-312-36794-5

Book design by David Mack and Kathleen Breitenfeld

First Edition: September 2007

For my mother Ida Mack,
and my aunt Evelyn Smith,
both grade-school teachers,
who introduced me to books and stories, and encouraged
my childhood art, curiosity, and strange notions.

To my father Wilson Mack,
for his stories and genetic material.

And to my brother and fellow creature, Steven.

Once upon a time,
there was a very shy girl.

She had a very shy dog,
and a very shy cat.
And a very shy fish,
who lived in a very high dish.

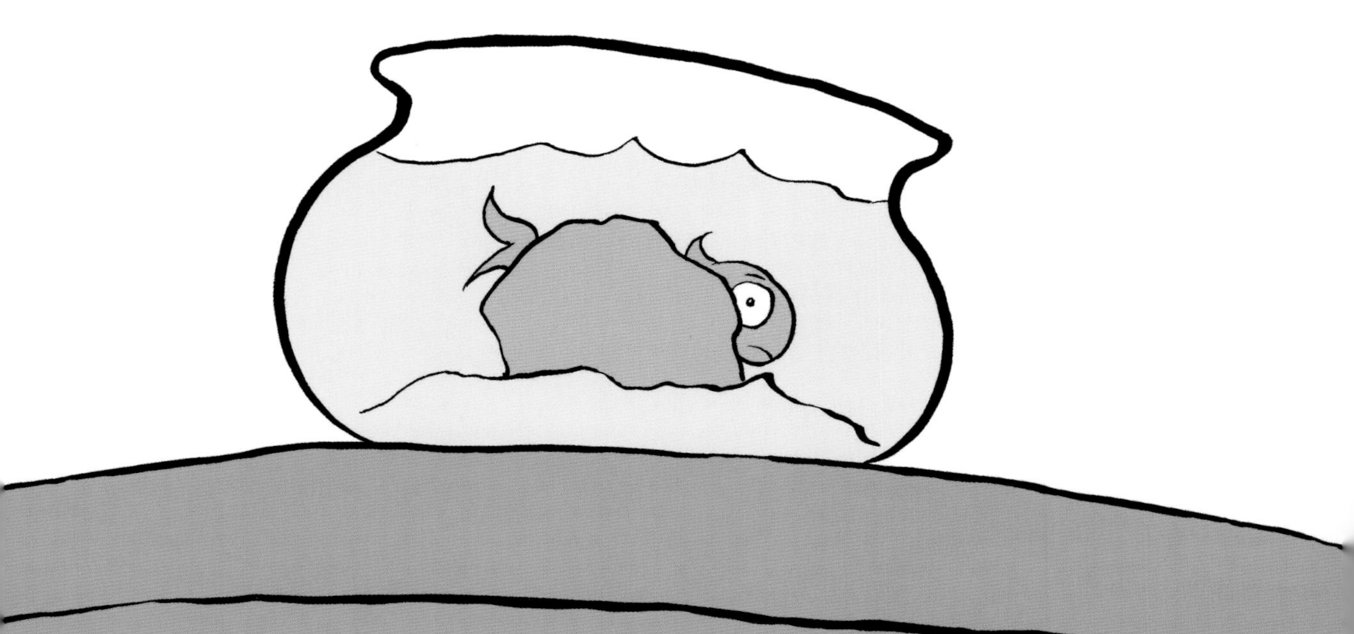

"It's really more of a bowl,"
the fish said.
Or he would have,
if he wasn't so shy.

One day in school,
the teacher asked
the shy girl's class,
"What do you want to be
when you grow up?"

"A doctor," said Larry.
"A fireman," said Terry.
"A teacher," said Mary.

"I want to be a doctor
to the shy creatures,"
said the shy girl.
Or she would have,
if she wasn't so shy.

"HA HA HA!"
the children might have laughed,
if the shy girl said what she might have said,
if she wasn't so shy instead.

"What do you mean?"
the teacher might sigh.

"What about Bigfoot?"
the shy girl would explain.

"What if Bigfoot stubbed his big toe?
That could cause a lot of pain!"

"Bigfoot isn't real,"
the teacher might say.

"That's no reason to ignore him!"
the shy girl would cry.
"Maybe he is real.
Maybe he's just shy."

"What if the Loch Ness Monster were to get a sore neck?

I could rub it for her,
and make her take a hot bath."

"HA HA HA!" the class would laugh.

"What if from breathing all that fire,
a Dragon's throat got sore?"

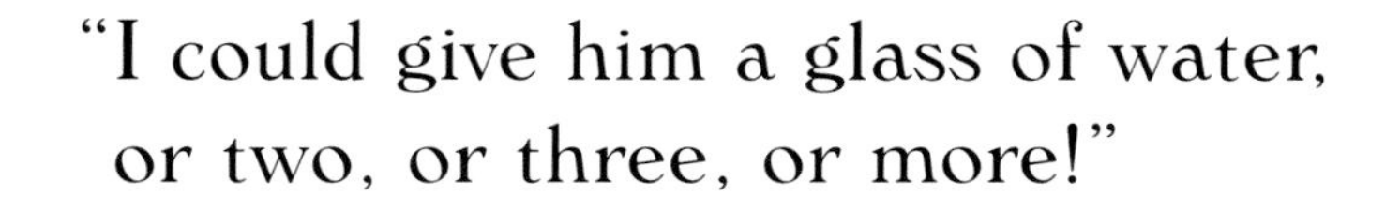

"I could give him a glass of water,
or two, or three, or more!"

"What if a Phoenix got itchy,
when rising from the ashes?

I could give her some lotion,
to help with any rashes."

SKIN CARE
cream

“What if Pegasus strained a wing?
I could put it in a sling.”

"What if the Cyclops
was nearsighted?"

"I could make him glasses!
I think he'd be delighted!"

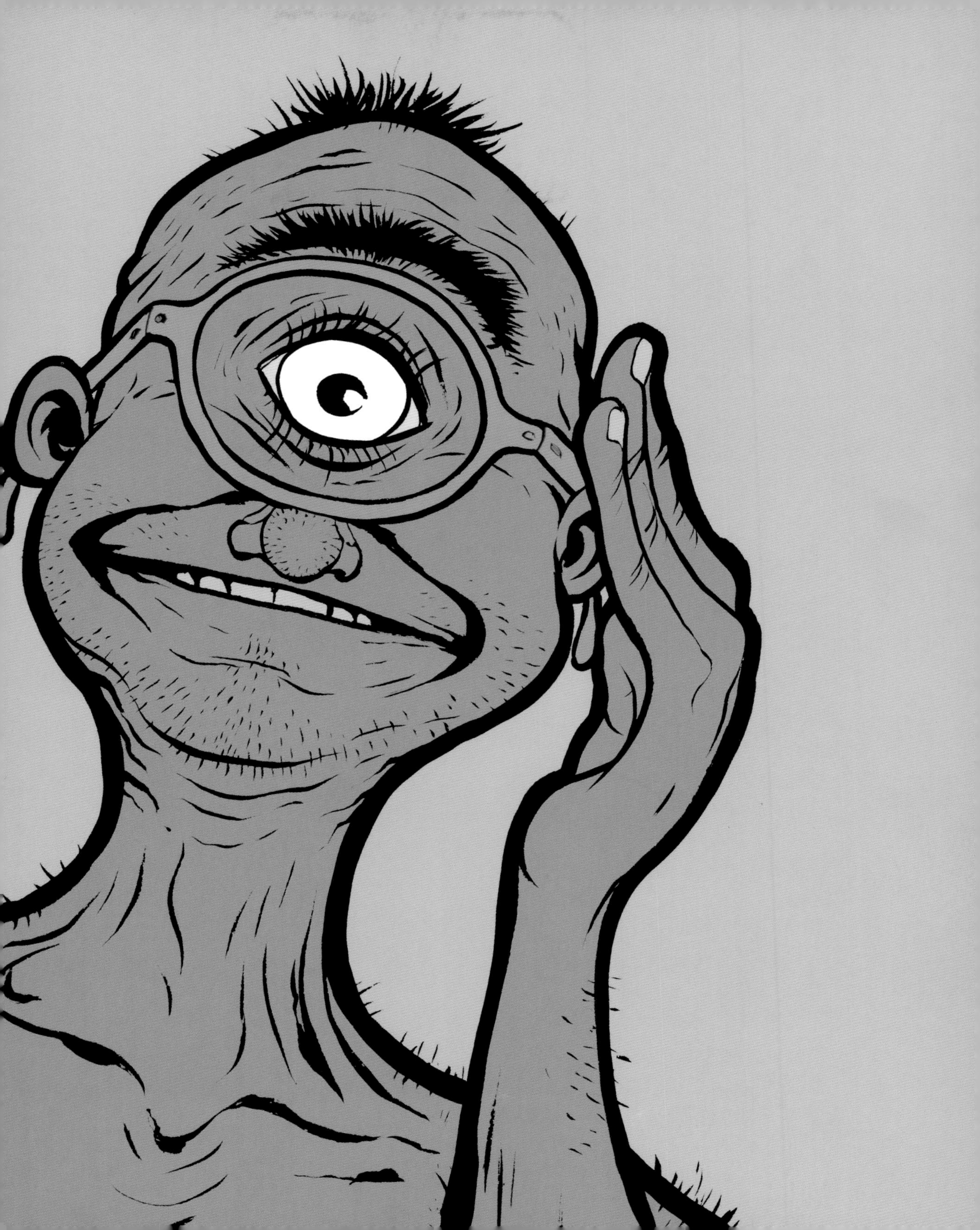

“What if the Pushmi-pullyu gets whiplash?

A neckbrace would
make him better in a flash!"

"HA HA HA!"
the class would laugh.

"What if Grey Aliens got eye boogers
in their great big eyes?
They could eat those
big alien boogers with fries!"

"OOOOOH! Gross!"
the class would cry!

"But what if the Chupacabra
got a toothache because he forgot
to brush his teeth?
What if they all fell out
so he couldn't eat?"

"I could make him a set of dentures
to get fed.
Then he could eat my vegetables
instead."

"Good idea!"
the class would have said.

"What if the Abominable Snowman overheated?
A haircut might be all he needed."

"I could clean him up just right
so he wouldn't give people such a fright!"

"But instead of a doctor,
what if the shy creatures
just needed a friend?
Then this story wouldn't
have to end!

All the shy creatures could
play games together,
like cards, and leapfrog,
and...whatever!"

"HA HA HA!"
the creatures would yell.

"HA HA HA!"
the class would laugh.

"HA HA HA!"
the shy girl cried.